7/13
1 —

ROBLOX MEETS MINECRAFT DIARY
#2

Legal Notice

Roblox Meets Minecraft Diary #2

A Diary of Two Worlds Colliding

Steve Robert

Contents

Friday

Well, the last few days have been quite the rollercoaster for us. Bob and I went from trying to find a few new decorations for my house to suddenly meeting Nick, the lost inmate from Roblox. This is definitely not how we expected this day to go.

Also, everything was made much worse when I had to go and meet Jack the Wizard again. He and I really don't get along. And now, I've become his little grocery haul guy. When we went to see him at his home, he gave us this massive list of things that we are now supposed to get for him.

He said that he needs to use these things in order to open a portal for Nick to go back into his world. I am really not sure how much Jack actually knows, or whether or not he has ever done something like this before. However, it really does not seem like we have any choice in the matter.

Bob and I certainly don't know how to open a portal into another universe, and Nick

doesn't even know which universe he is currently in! This whole thing has made us very stressed out indeed. Although, if anyone can do this, it's Jack the Wizard.

I may not be his biggest fan, but I've seen him do some weird things over the years, and I don't remember that he has ever failed before. So, if there is anyone who can truly help us in this matter, it is going to be the wizard.

However, one of the problems that I am now facing is that his list of ingredients that he says he needs is almost ridiculous. Weird, plants, bats, tools, certain things that can only be collected at a specific time of day. It's a very strange position to be in.

And to make things worse, Nick and Bob don't look too thrilled about the process either. I am sure that they were looking forward to just getting Jack the Wizard to quickly open a new portal before they simply move on with their lives. But, sadly, that is not the case today.

Plus, we were starting to get hungry. When we left Jack's house, we rushed out because

we were excited to get started with collecting the ingredients. However, it has now been long enough without any proper food, so we're going to need to stop by somewhere to eat.

"Are you guys hungry?" I asked my other two travelers.

"I'm starving, to be honest," said Nick. "I don't even remember the last time I ate."

"Same," said Bob. "I think it's time we stop by somewhere for a snack."

"Where do you guys want to go?" I asked.

"I don't know any places here," said Nick.

"We can grab some burgers over at the Burger Place," said Bob.

I thought about it for a moment. It has been a long time since we went to the Burger Place. It's a small restaurant that one of Bob's friends made when he was craving some new kind of food. It turned out to be a popular place where creatures of all kinds get together.

"That sounds like a great idea," I said.

"Let's go."

So, we made our way to the Burger Place. It would take us a while to walk there, but I guess we were so hungry that we didn't really mind how long it would actually take as long as there is any food at the end of the line.

I wondered if Nick would like the kind of food that we eat here. I also wondered if they had the same kind of food over where he lives.

"Do you have burgers in your dimension?" I asked Nick.

"Oh yeah," said Nick. "I love those. Used to have them all the time before I went to prison."

I then realized that I had completely forgotten about Nick going to prison at all. I was stuck in the thought that we were just randomly going to send him back home and that would be the end of it all.

"What kind of food did you have in the

prison?" asked Bob.

"Mostly different kinds of stew," said Nick. "They fill you up, but I can tell you, they are anything but delicious. It takes a long time to get used to everything."

I thought about this for a moment. It must have been very difficult for Nick to get used to this new life in prison must not have been easy at all. And it is even worse for him because he was wrongfully accused of something that he did not do. I don't know how he managed it.

"I hope you will enjoy our version of burgers. They might be a little weird when you first see them," I said.

"I wouldn't worry about it to be honest," said Nick. "I am so hungry right now that I can pretty much eat anything in sight!"

"Yeah, I understand that feeling," added Bob.

So we continued to walk towards the Burger Place. I hadn't been there in a long time, but I was wondering if it still looked and smelled the same as when I remembered it.

Eventually, we approached the small hill on top of which was the Burger Place. We could already see that there were other creatures lining up to eat. I was worried that we would have to wait a long time before we got our own chance to enter the place.

"We're going to have to get in line," I said.

"Not necessarily," said Bob. "I know a few creatures inside who might be willing to give us an empty seat somewhere inside."

"Since when were you the social butterfly?" I asked Bob.

"I haven't been a social butterfly for a long time," he replied, "but when my stomach is rumbling, I like to have a few friends in the right place so that I can get to the food quicker."

"That's good to know," I said.

I hadn't seen Bob this excited in a very long time. I guess the whole adventure thing and the fact that we had been walking around for a long time had taken its toll on his appetite. I have to admit that I feel the same way. I couldn't wait to get near a burger.

When we entered the Burger Place, it was completely jam-packed. There was not a single free chair in sight. Everything was overtaken by a variety of creatures, all munching down on what seem like endless varieties of burgers.

The great thing about the Burger Place is that they were so good at mixing all of the various ingredients and allowing you to choose what kind of burger you wanted to have. I personally always enjoyed the simplest possible version, but it was good to know that we could get creative.

Bob then walked up to the bar. Another skeleton was working behind it. He recognized Bob immediately and waved at him. Bob approached the bar and exchanged a few words with the other skeleton. Nick and I decided to stay behind so as not to accidentally ruin the mood.

"Do you know that other guy?" Nick asked me.

"No, I've never seen him before," I said. "I figure it's better if we stay here and wait for

Bob to figure it out. I don't want us to seem to needy."

"Agreed," said Nick.

We waited a little longer on the side while waiting for Bob to finish the conversation. The more we looked at all the others around us having burgers, the hungrier we were getting. I almost couldn't wait to get my hands on an actual burger!

Finally, Bob started making his way back towards us. I was so happy to see him coming, because I really don't know how much longer I could have waited without getting any food!

"Good news guys," said Bob. "My friend over there is going to give us a great table and we can stay as long as we want! It's usually super crowded here, but me and that other guy go way back, so this is now a great chance for us to have a proper meal."

"Finally!" I exclaimed.

"Thank you so much!" said Nick.

Then, I saw the other skeleton at the bar

motion towards a table in the corner. He obviously wanted us to go over there and to take a seat.

"I guess that's out queue," said Bob.

Quickly, all three of us made out way to the table and we immediately sat down and grabbed the menus. No one spoke to anyone else for a while, because we were trying to figure out what kind of burger we wanted, and what we wanted to get on the side.

There were so many choices to choose from! Regular cheeseburgers with extra fries, and then also some weird things like seaweed burgers. I really didn't want to try anything that I didn't already know the taste of.

By the looks of it, Bob and Nick were thinking the same thing. This was not the right time to experiment with food. We could do that another time when we were not so hungry. Also, I already knew that there would be a huge adventure ahead of us, and there was no point going into an adventure hungry!

Finally, we all made our choices.

"I'll have a double cheeseburger with extra fried," said Bob.

"Me too," said Nick.

"I'll join you and I'll add a chocolate milkshake too," I replied.

When the waiter came, we made our order, and then prepared for the wait before our burgers would finally arrive.

I decided to get our minds off of the food a little by looking through the list of ingredients that the wizard had given us one more time. Perhaps we could come up with some sort of plan which would help us to gather the ingredients quicker.

"We want to make sure that we don't waste too much time going back and forth to different places," said Bob. "We need to make sure that we gather as many of the ingredients as we possibly can in one place before we move onto another. Otherwise I would be worried that Nick will end up being stuck here."

"You're right," I said. "I'm going to divide

the ingredients into categories. This way, we will know exactly what we need to look for when we reach a specific location. The sooner we get back to the wizard, the sooner we can get that portal opened!"

"I am really looking forward to that," said Nick. "Please don't get me wrong, I really appreciate you guys and also this dimension. But I just won't feel at home until I am actually back home."

"Don't worry, we understand," said Bob. "You don't have to apologize. Let's munch down on these burgers and then get you home as quickly as possible."

Just then, the burgers had finally arrived. The waiter placed one burger in front of each one of us, and also added our drinks and the fries on the side. Everything looks so delicious!

We spent a long time just eating the food and not thinking about anything else. It was actually a relief to not have to feel stressed about anything for a while and to just enjoy the burger. Even Nick looked like he had

temporarily forgotten that he was in another dimension.

Once we finished the burgers, we sat back and took some time to rest from this delicious meal.

"This was amazing," said Nick.

"Yup," was all that Bob could say.

I couldn't even say that, so I just decided to stay quiet and to enjoy the moment while it still lasted. Soon, we would have to leave this place and start our way into a very difficult journey of searching for ingredients.

Although I was definitely happy to look for them and to get Nick back home, I was not looking forward to all of the scary things that could happen to us along the way. However, there was no other way to go about the situation that we were currently finding ourselves in, other than to get on with it.

So, when we finished all of our burgers, we paid and thanked the waiter. Then, we got ready to head on out to a whole new

adventure. Maybe we shouldn't have eaten as much as we had because we were feeling s little sluggish…

Saturday

Wooo yesterday was quite the adventure!

Even getting the very first item on the list was a huge challenge for us, and one that we were certainly not prepared for. But we made it anyway.

What happened was that we started our journey into the forest. The reason why we did this is because we needed to gather a very special kind of mushrooms first. I had never heard of these mushrooms before, and they were supposed to be pink in color.

As soon as we entered the forest, we knew that this would quickly become a difficult task because we had no idea where to start looking for it. So, in an effort to speed up the process, we decided to split up.

I was a little worried about Nick, because he

had never been into this forest before, but then I remembered that I had never been in it either, so we were sort of all on the same ground.

"Are you going to be ok on your own?" I asked Nick.

"Oh yeah, don't worry about it," he replied. "If anything happens I'll give you guys a shout."

I looked over at Bob with some concern because I was not sure how much I could trust that Nick was brave enough to go and look for the mushrooms entirely on his own.

"I don't think we have anything to worry about," said Bob. "We won't separate too far from one another, so if something does happen we will be able to hear one another call for help."

I thought about it a little longer and then I decided that Bob was probably right. We needed to have certain faith in each other if this whole thing was going to work out. So, we entered the forest and immediately went our separate ways.

Looking for a cute little pink mushroom turned out to be a lot more difficult than I thought it would be. I had to enter really deep into the forest, and the more I moved inside the darker the forest became. Soon, I lost sight of Bob and Nick. I could only hope that they were also safe, and having a better time looking for the mushroom.

I carefully walked through the forest and really kept my eyes down to the bottom of the trees where the mushrooms grow. I saw a few of the regular mushrooms which I have seen many times before, but there was just no sign of the super special pink mushrooms that we were looking for.

Then, I saw a turtle slowly, very slowly, try and walk up towards me. I didn't notice it before, but it genuinely looked like it was out breath. I decided to wait for it to approach me, since there was no one else looking at it in the forest at the moment.

Then, the turtle practically shouted at me!

"Heeeeey…" the turtle tried to shout but it was seriously out of breath. "I've been chasing you for an hour…."

"Huh?" I said. "You've been… chasing me? What for?"

"Jack said to come get you…!" said the turtle.

I was very confused at this point. A turtle was out of breath trying to reach me.

"Jack sent a turtle… to chase me?" I said.

Finally, the turtle managed to reach me.

"He ain't bright," said the turtle.

I gave the turtle a few moments to compose itself, because it seemed t really be having a hard time catching its breath.

"Why did he send you?" I asked.

"He said that you would never find the mushrooms without me. Also, all the other animals are doing something else so I was the only one left that that dumb wizard could send. I can't breathe!" shouted the turtle.

"I mean, it's a mushroom," I said. "And it's pink, how difficult can it be to find? It's going to stand out from all the other mushrooms in this forest for sure."

"Yah," said the turtle, "but you're not going to look for it where you're supposed to. I need to take you to it."

Already, I noticed that we were about to enter into a whole new kind of problem. Can you imagine how long it would take for a turtle to show me where to find a mushroom?

"Can't you just show me where to go?" I asked the turtle.

"No," it said. "I didn't come all the way here just to point in one direction. We're going together."

With no other option, I had to walk alongside the turtle and hope that wherever we were going wasn't an entire lifetime away.

"Is it really far away where we're going? I do need to speed this up, you know. I want to get Nick back to his world as soon as possible," I told the turtle.

"No, no don't worry," replied the turtle. "It's not that far at all, I just want to be part of

this so that I can brag about today when I get back home to the wife and kids."

I sort of understood where he was coming from, and I did hope that he would get a good story out of all this, but I was still worried about how long we had to go to reach the correct spot. Walking with a turtle is a really slow process that could take days if you're not careful!

But, I guess we were both in this together, and so we needed a way to support each other. After all, it must be quite boring to be a turtle. It takes a long time to collect any fun stories to tell your friends, so I guess at least now he could have one.

"What do we do when we reach the place with the mushrooms?" I asked.

"You pick as many as Jack told you to, but you don't pick any more than that," said the turtle. "These are very special mushrooms that we're looking for and they take a very long time to grow. We cannot take more than we were asked to."

"This is the easiest task on the list," I said. "I

44

have no idea how I'm going to get all of the other things that I was asked to."

"Well, even this may not be as easy as you think," said the turtle.

At first, I had no idea what he meant. But then, as we approached the place where the pink mushrooms were, I realized that he was right.

As soon as we approached the huge tree, the turtle exclaimed that we had finally made it to the place where the pink mushrooms grow.

"Here we are," said the turtle.

I looked at the bottom of the tree, but I couldn't see any mushrooms around it. Then I walked around the tree, but still no luck. There were no mushrooms to be found at all.

"Where are they?" I asked the turtle.

The turtle then pointed up towards the top of the tree. I raised my head and immediately knew that I now had a serious problem to deal with.

The pink mushrooms, which I was expecting

to find at the bottom of the tree like you would find any other mushroom, were in fact at the very top of tree. In fact, the only reason why I could see them was because they were super bright pink in color.

"How am I supposed to get up there?" I asked the turtle.

"No idea," he replied.

"So why are you even here then?" I asked again.

"That's my adventure story. Watching you struggle, and maybe even fall from the tree will be my adventure story that I get to take back with me!" exclaimed the turtle.

"You could have at least told me to get the others for some help!" I said, annoyed.

But the turtle simple made his way to another tree and then relaxed, and watched me try and deal with this new struggle. I was really not expecting to be treated like this. And by no less than a turtle!

I looked around me but I knew immediately that the other guys would not be able to hear

me if I called them. Even though we promised that we would not go too far away from each other, I had actually gone to far, and now no one would be able to hear me properly when I call.

So, this means that I had no other choice but to figure out a way to climb that tree on my own and to get all of the mushrooms.

The good news is that I was surrounded by trees and many green plants. This also means that there were many vines around me, which I could sort of use to climb the tree. But it would definitely be dangerous. I haven't done something like this since I was very small, so I had no idea if I remembered how to do it properly or if I could get hurt.

"I hope you're watching!" I yelled over to the turtle.

"Oh, I am!" he replied.

I moved around a little more to look for the perfect vine. I got the idea from looking at the tree that I was supposed to climb, and I

immediately realized that the only way to do it was with the help of a vine.

The tree was tall and very old, and it didn't have any branches lower at the bottom of the tree, which means that I had nothing to hang on to on my way up. Soon, I finally found the perfect vine that could help me with this job.

I took the vine from another tree and then brought it back to the mushroom tree. Then, I placed the vine around the tree and held it tight with both hands. I made sure that I had a good grip, because if I let go of the vine at any moment, I would probably fall.

"Slow and steady!" yelled the turtle.

"Yeah, you would know," I replied.

Then, I had no other choice but to start climbing. I started off very slowly, because I wanted to make sure that I learn to do it properly before I go way too high up in the tree. After a few movements upwards, I became used to using the vine.

Luckily, the big tree was very dry, which helped to keep the vine stable and to give it

a good hold on the tree. I was seriously hoping that this vine was going to hold on until I reached the top. How I would then come down, I had no idea.

I slowly kept moving up and up without ever looking down. I was scared that if I looked down I would become too scared and freeze in the middle of a very tall tree. Slowly, I reached one of the first branches where I could hold on.

I grabbed the branch and made my way on top of it. Eventually, I was able to actually sit on the branch and rest my hands. I still did not dare to look down, I only took a look at how far the pink mushrooms were from me now.

They were actually much closer then I thought, which at least made me a little happy. Slowly, I moved towards the pink mushrooms. I wrapped the vine around my waist for later when I come down.

Right now I had enough branches to work with. So I slowly climbed from one branch to another, until I finally reached the pink mushrooms. There were so man of them on

the top of this tree! I knew that I didn't need all of them. Luckily, a single branch had enough of these mushrooms for what I needed.

When I reached the mushrooms, I slowly plucked them and put them in my pockets. One by one, I made sure not to break the mushrooms as I plucked them. Because I really didn't want to have to come back here and do all of this again!

When I had enough mushrooms to work with, I zipped up my pockets, and then prepared to make my way down the tree. I was really not looking forward to this, but at least I knew that going down the tree would mean that I would eventually reach the ground and be safe again.

I used the same vine, and very slowly made my way down the tree. Step by step, I held on to the vine and climbed down. It took a little less time than it did to climb the tree, but it was very stressful and my hands were starting to hurt.

I was delighted when I finally made it down to the ground! I looked at the turtle. He was

smiling at me. He looked like he was glad that I made it, but he also looked happy that he had a story to tell.

"Well, I didn't fall from the tree," I said to the turtle.

"No," he replied. "It's a good thing you didn't because that would have been a very bad fall!"

"Are you coming back with me?" I asked.

"No, I live just round the corner. I'll be laving you here," he said.

"Well, thanks for your help I guess. Even though you let me climb that dangerous tree all on my own!" I replied.

"Good luck with the mushrooms!" yelled the turtle. Then, he made his way back to his own home.

I had no other choice but to make my way back, and hope that I would once again find Bob and Nick somewhere in the forest. Hopefully they didn't go too far away so that I can't reach them. I also wondered if they had a similar adventure that I had.

Then, I saw them in the distance!

Bob and Nick had somehow found each other, and it was obvious that they were looking for me. I couldn't hear them shouting yet because they were so far away, but I could see them coming my way in the distance.

"Hey!" I shouted. "Over here!" I waved my hands as much as I could in order to grab their attention. I didn't want them to leave anywhere without me. This forest was starting to feel a little creepy.

As I approached them, I realized that they were also carrying pink mushrooms. How strange! And also, how did they get them? Did all pink mushrooms grow high up in the trees?

Finally, we met each other half way through the forest.

"Steve!" shouted Nick. "We've been looking for you for ages!"

"Same here!" I said. "Where have you guys been? And are those pink mushrooms? How

did you get them?"

"Oh, we met a few turtles along the way who showed us the trees where the pink mushrooms grow. Unfortunately, they grow super high up and we both had to climb up to get them. How did you get the mushrooms?" asked Bob.

"Same thing," I replied. "I met a turtle that showed me the way and I also had to climb a tree. I was so scared."

"So it's just turtles showing people the way through the forest?" asked Nick.

"Guess so," I replied. "I was a little annoyed with the turtle at first to be honest. But now that I think about it, I never would have thought that these mushrooms would be growing on top of a tree!"

"We thought the same thing," said Bob. "I never would have figured it out on my own. I've never before seen mushrooms that grow so high up."

"Well, at least we got them I guess," said Nick. "But this is only one of the things that we needed to get. There are many more

things left on the list."

He was right. There really were many more things left on the list to get, and I had no idea how long it would take us to do it, or how difficult it would be. Would we have to climb a new tree for every new ingredient that we needed?

Probably not, but this was definitely going to be even harder than we thought it was going to be. Which means that we had a long way to go and that also needed to be careful not to get hurt. All of these things were so important to think of if we ever had a chance of getting Nick back home in one piece.

"Well boys," said Bob. "Looks like we are going to have to move faster than before if we are to get this job done in time."

He was right. There were so many other things that we would have to think of, and we haven't even made it to that point yet. For now, we needed to regroup and to see what the next item on the long list of ingredients was going to be.

Slowly, we walked our way out of the forest and towards the sea. The next ingredient was a very weird-looking fish. Who knows how this adventure was going to end, so we needed to hurry up. Otherwise, I was worried that Nick would end up staying here forever if we cannot bring him back to his own dimension.

Time for another adventure!

66

Made in the USA
Las Vegas, NV
18 December 2020